To All the Little Blamers Out There!
~Love, Julia

But It's Not My Fault

Written by
Julia Cook

Illustrated by
Anita DuFalla

But It's Not My Fault
Text and Illustrations Copyright © 2015 by Father Flanagan's Boys' Home
ISBN 978-1-934490-80-8

Published by the Boys Town Press
14100 Crawford St.
Boys Town, NE 68010

For a Boys Town Press catalog, call **1-800-282-6657**
or visit our website: **BoysTownPress.org**

Publisher's Cataloging-in-Publication Data

Cook, Julia, 1964-

But it's not my fault! / written by Julia Cook ; illustrated by Anita DuFalla. – Boys Town, NE :
Boys Town Press, [2015]

    pages ; cm.
    (Responsible me!)

    ISBN: 978-1-934490-80-8
    Audience: grades K-6.
    Summary: Shows readers how to accept responsibility for their actions and not blame or try to find fault with others.–Publisher.

    1. Children–Life skills guides–Juvenile fiction. 2. Responsibility in children–Juvenile fiction. 3. Honesty–Juvenile fiction. 4. Blame–Juvenile fiction. 5. Faultfinding–Juvenile fiction. 6. Child psychology. 7. [Conduct of life–Fiction. 8. Responsibility–Fiction. 9. Honesty–Fiction. 10. Blame--Fiction. 11. Behavior.] I. DuFalla, Anita. II. Title. III. Series.

PZ7.C76984 B88 2015

E   1503

Printed in the United States
10 9 8 7 6 5

Boys Town Press is the publishing division of Boys Town, a national organization serving children and families.

My name is
Norman David Edwards...
but everybody calls me
"Noodle."

Sometimes things
happen to me that
get me into trouble.

But it's not my fault.

Things just aren't the way they should bc.
I feel like everybody's always picking on me!
I always get blamed and it's not my fault.
Seems like I'm the only one that ever gets caught!

Yesterday, I didn't get my math homework done. So this morning, my teacher made me stay in from recess and do it... RaTS!

But it wasn't my fault!

Last night I had to go to my big brother's basketball game, and it went into overtime, and by the time I finally got home, it was too late to do my homework so my **MOM** made me go to bed.

After recess, we all headed to the library to work on our science reports. Since my **TEACHER** wouldn't let me go to recess, I had lots of extra energy. I felt kinda twitchy. On the way down the hall, I jumped up high and tried to touch the light. On the way down, **MARY GOLD** got in my airspace and her head hit my arm.

"Ouch!

Teacher... Noodle hit me!"

"But it's not my fault!

YOU didn't let me go out to recess,
and my legs just needed to jump.
It wasn't my fault, my arm did it.
And it was just a little bump."

I got sent to the end of the line... RATS!

7

Then, when I got to the library, I couldn't work on my report on the duck-billed platypus because the **MEDIA SPECIALIST** wouldn't let me check out the book that I needed!

"Noodle, you can't check out a new book until you bring your overdue book back."

Duck-Billed Platypus

BOOK RETURN

"But it's not my fault!"

"I looked in my backpack this morning
as soon as I got to school.
My **MOM** didn't remind me to put it in there,
so please, can you bend the rules?"

"NOPE!"

In PE, **ROSS GREY** tripped me on purpose and then he laughed at me when I fell down... so I pushed him over.

"Teacher... Noodle pushed me!"

"But it's not my fault!

ROSS GREY tripped me on purpose, and that made me really feel bad. And then he laughed when I fell, which made me really **MAD!**"

Noodle DID IT!

He did it AGAIN!

My hands were **so mad** that they pushed him,
even though my brain told them not to!

Things just aren't the way they should be.
I feel like everybody's always picking on me!
I always get blamed
and it's not my fault.
Seems like I'm the only one
that ever gets caught!

"Noodle! Please STOP TALKING!"

"But it's not my fault. GEORGIE talked to me first!"

"Noodle! Please stop LOLLYGAGGING!"

"But it's not my fault, I was born this way! Besides... the pencil sharpener needed to be emptied."

"Noodle! You just **interrupted again!**"

"But it's not my fault!

My mouth is addicted to talking!"

"Noodle! We don't stick our tongue **out** at other kids!"

"But it's not my fault!

T.J. did it to me first and then he stared at me, so I had to do it back to him.

Besides, it doesn't say we can't do that in the school handbook!"

Just as my teacher was about to say "Noodle" for the **fifty thousandth time,** the bell rang.

Whew!

"Noodle," my teacher said. "Please stay after for a minute so we can have a talk."

"RaTs!"

"Noodle, today you had a really rough day."

"But it's not my fault!"

"Noodle... there are no 'BUTS' in my sentence.

Today you had a really rough day **AND** tomorrow is a **brand new day!** I can't wait to see what you can do with your tomorrow! Have a safe walk home."

When I walked into my house, my mom gave me the **"unibrow."** I could tell just by the way she looked at me that I was in trouble.... RaTS!

"Noodle, your teacher emailed me and told me that today at school you had a really rough day!"

"But it's not my fault!"

"I didn't get my homework done because the game went late and **YOU** made me to go to bed.

My **TEACHER** wouldn't let me go out to recess, and my legs needed to jump.

MARY GOLD got in my airspace and her head hit my arm!

I couldn't do my report on the duck-billed platypus because the **MEDIA SPECIALIST** wouldn't let me check out the book I needed because **YOU** forgot to remind me to put my overdue book in my backpack this morning!"

HOMEWORK

Duck-Billed Platypus

"**ROSS GREY** tripped me and laughed when I fell down and that made my hands **mad!**

GEORGIE talked to me first!

The pencil sharpener needed to be emptied.

My mouth is addicted to talking.

And it doesn't say in the school handbook that I can't stick my tongue out at people. Besides, I had to! **T.J.** was staring at me!

And he did it to me first!"

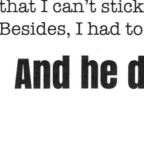

Things just aren't the way they should be.
I feel like everybody's always picking on me!

I always get blamed and **it's not my fault.**
Seems like I'm the only one that ever gets caught!

"Noodle! I'm not talking about whose

fault

it is," mom said.

"I'm talking about whose

responsibility

it is."

"Huh???"

"**YOU** are responsible for the things that you do.
For your choices at home and your choices at school!
Blaming others is a reason, but it's not an excuse.
If you keep playing this game, **YOU** surely will lose!"

"YOU are in charge of letting me know when you have homework!

YOU are in charge of returning **YOUR** library books!"

"And **YOU** are in charge

of your legs,
your **arms**,
your hands,
your **voice...**
and your **tongue!**

Today, you made a few mistakes,
and it caused your day to be rough.
But don't blame others for your poor choices,
because that will make your life tough.

Instead focus on what needs to be done,
whenever you make a mistake.
Own up and become more responsible
for the choices that you've made."

"Noodle, everybody makes mistakes and mistakes can be a good thing because every time you make one, it gives you a chance to learn something!" mom said.

"If you blame other people for your mistakes, you give away your chances to learn!

Don't make an excuse when you do something wrong.

Just own it and say,

'Yep!
I did that!
Now what can I do to improve my situation?'"

PROBLEM-SOLVING WAND

"Noodle, I love you with all of my heart, and I wish I could solve all of your problems for you, but I can't.

My job is to teach you to become your own **problem-solver.**"

"The next time you make a mistake,
on the inside think, **'Yep, that was me.'**
It's going to be hard but like everyone says,
'The **good stuff in life** is not free!'

If you're brave enough to own your mistakes,
imagine how **GREAT** you'll become!
You'll learn a lot, you'll make better choices,
and your life will be **SO MUCH more fun!**

Don't be a blamer, you're better than that.
Use your mistakes to help you grow.

Get rid of the phrase,

'But it's not my fault!'

and show the world how much you know."

Maybe my mom was right.

Maybe I was blaming others for my mistakes.

Yep, I guess I did make a few wrong choices today....

As soon as I got to school the next day, I went to the library, turned in my overdue book, and checked out the book I needed for my report on the duck-billed platypus.

When I walked into my classroom, my teacher put her arm around me and whispered,

"Noodle, yesterday you had a really rough day, and today is a brand new day. I can't wait to see what you can do with your today."

27

Then she said, "Class, it's time for me to collect the rough drafts of your science papers."

When she got to my desk, I said,

"I don't have mine done... but it's... but it's... but it's gonna be done by tomorrow morning. I just checked out the book that I needed."

Duck-Billed Platypus

Way To Go Noodle!

"YOU DID IT!!!

You took responsibility for your actions!
I am **SO** proud of how brave you are!

As a reward, I'm going to give you an
extra day to get your rough draft done!
When you hand it in tomorrow,
it won't be counted late."

29

30

Conquering the BLAME GAME!

Teaching children to accept responsibility for their actions is a learned behavior that is VITAL to character development. Children don't just grow out of the natural tendencies to blame others and/or shirk responsibility. In fact, if these behaviors are not effectively addressed early on, they become self-reinforcing and will likely dramatically increase into adulthood.

Here are a few tips that might help curb the "BLAME GAME"

1. The consequences for making responsible choices should be highly motivating for your children, while blaming others and making excuses should result in negative consequences that are highly demotivating.

2. Explain to your child that everyone makes mistakes. Mistakes are a good thing because every time children make one, it gives them a chance to learn something. When they blame others for their mistakes, they give away their chances to learn!

3. Don't overreact when your child blames others or makes excuses for poor choices. If you keep your cool, your child will be more apt to focus on his or her own behavior rather than reacting to yours.

4. If your child makes a poor choice, try not to nag or give excessive warnings. Instead, remain emotionally neutral and follow through with the appropriate consequences. In a nutshell, don't let your child drain your energy!

5. If your child tries to argue with you or acts insincere, set a timer for three minutes and walk away. Explain to your child that you will come back when the timer goes off and discuss the situation with him or her, but you will not argue. Set your boundaries and stick to them. This gives your child a few minutes to internally process the situation, own it, and organize a more suitable response. It also allows your child to develop effective autonomy.

6. Be very consistent in your responses and reactions. Children need to be well aware of the boundaries that apply to their world, and know what the consequences will be if they choose to violate them.

7. With older children and teens, explain that appropriate choices yield appropriate privileges, including getting to use the car, hanging out with friends, having access to technology, enjoying activities, etc. The more responsible your child is, the more privileges he or she can enjoy. Remind your children that they have control over their quality of life, and then let them make the choices that will yield either privileges or negative consequences.

8. When children make a poor choice, coach them toward accepting responsibility by expecting them to clearly vocalize what they did, explain how it was hurtful or irresponsible, and apologize. Then, help them identify what a better choice might have been.

9. Model productive behavior!!! You are your child's coping instructor. Stop seeing your child as a victim. Don't blame external situations for his or her individual predicament.

Remember... it's not about "fault," it's about responsibility!

For more parenting information, visit boystown.org/parenting.

BOYS TOWN. Parenting

Boys Town Press Books by Julia Cook
Kid-friendly stories to teach social skills

Responsible ME!

A book series to help kids take responsibility for their behavior.

978-1-934490-80-8

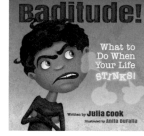
978-1-934490-90-7

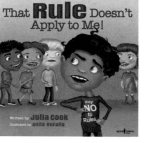
978-1-934490-98-3

978-1-944882-08-2

978-1-944882-09-9

978-1-934490-30-3

978-1-934490-47-1

978-1-934490-48-8

978-1-934490-86-0

978-1-934490-97-6

978-1-944882-05-1

Building RELATIONSHIPS

A book series to help kids get along.

Other Titles:
Cliques Just Don't Make Cents and *Hygiene You Stink!*

BEST ME I Can Be!

To reinforce the social skills RJ learns in each book, corresponding poster sets and activity guides are available.

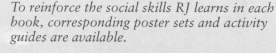

COMMUNICATE with Confidence

A book series to help kids master the art of communicating.

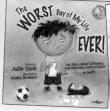
978-1-934490-20-4

978-1-934490-43-3

978-1-934490-49-5

978-1-934490-67-9

Other Titles: *Teamwork Isn't My Thing, and I Don't Like to Share!*, *I Just Don't Like the Sound of NO!* and *Sorry, I Forgot to Ask!*

978-1-934490-57-0

978-1-934490-58-7

978-1-944882-13-6

Other Title: *Gas Happens!*

BOYS TOWN Press®

BoysTownPress.org

For information on Boys Town, its Education Model®, Common Sense Parenting®, and training programs:
boystowntraining.org | boystown.org/parenting
training@BoysTown.org | 1-800-545-5771

For parenting and educational books and other resources:
BoysTownPress.org
btpress@BoysTown.org | 1-800-282-6657